THE RIVER GOD

BY

ROLAND PERTWEE

British Library Cataloguing-in-Publication Data
A catalogue record for this book is available from the
British Library

CONTENTS

ROLAND PERTWEE.. 1

THE RIVER GOD 3

ROLAND PERTWEE

Roland Pertwee was born in Brighton, England in 1885. Pertwee served in the Army during the First World War, before retiring to pursue a career in the flourishing British film industry. Between the 1910s and the 1950s, Pertwee worked as a writer on an array of films, including MGM's *A Yank at Oxford*, alongside F. Scott Fitzgerald. He also tried his hand at acting in as many as ten different productions. In 1954, along with his older son, Michael, Pertwee created *The Grove Family*, widely regarded as the first soap opera in the history of British television. At its height, *The Grove Family* is said to have been watched by in one in every four television owners in the country. Pertwee produced a number of works of juvenile fiction, but it was his two short stories, 'The River God' and 'Fish Are Such Liars', that earned him major critical acclaim. Both pieces are now considered classics of the short form, and were published posthumously, in 1970.

THE RIVER GOD

When I was a little boy I had a friend who was a colonel. He was not the kind of colonel you meet nowadays, who manages a motor showroom in the West End of London and wears crocodile shoes and a small moustache and who calls you 'old man' and slaps your back, independent of the fact that you may have been no more than a private in the war. My colonel was of the older order that takes a third of a century and a lot of Indian sun and Madras curry in the making.

A veteran of the Mutiny he was, and wore side whiskers to prove it.

Once he came upon a number of sepoys conspiring mischief in a byre with a barrel of gunpowder. So he put the butt of his cheroot into the barrel and presently they all went to hell. That was the kind of man he was in the way of business.

In the way of pleasure he was very different. In the way of pleasure he wore an old Norfolk coat that smelt of heather and brine, and which had no elbows to speak of. And he wore a Sherlock Holmesy kind of cap with a swarm of salmon flies upon it, that to my boyish fancy was more splendid than a crown. I cannot remember his legs, because they were nearly always under water, hidden in great canvas waders. But once he sent me a photograph of himself riding on a tricycle, so I expect he had some knickerbockers too, which would have been that tight kind, with box cloth under the knees.

Boys don't take much stock of clothes. His head occupied my imagination. A big, brave, white-haired head with cherry-red rugose cheeks and honest, laughing, puckered eyes, with gunpowder marks in their corners.

People at the little Welsh fishing inn where we met said he

was a bore; but I knew him to be a god and shall prove it.

I was ten years old and his best friend.

He was seventy something and my hero.

Properly I should not have mentioned my hero so soon in this narrative. He belongs to a later epoch, but sometimes it is forgivable to start with a boast, and now that I have committed myself I lack the courage to call upon my colonel to fall back two paces to the rear, quick march, and wait until he is wanted.

The real beginning takes place, as I remember, somewhere in Hampshire on the Grayshott Road, among sandy banks, sentinel firs, and plum-coloured wastes of heather. Summer holiday time it was, and I was among folks whose names have since vanished like lizards under the stones of forgetfulness.

Perhaps it was a picnic walk; perhaps I carried a basket and was told not to swing it for fear of bursting its cargo of ginger beer. In those days ginger beer had big bulgy corks held down with string. In a hot sun or under stress of too much agitation the string would break and the corks fly. Then there would be a merry foaming fountain and someone would get reproached.

One of our company had a fishing rod. He was a young man who, one day, was to be an uncle of mine. But that didn't concern me. What concerned me was the fishing rod, and presently – perhaps because he felt he must keep in with the family – he let me carry it.

To the fisherman born there is nothing so provoking of curiosity as a fishing rod in a case. Surreptitiously I opened the flap, which contained a small brass spear in a wee pocket, and, pulling down the case a little, I admired the beauties of the cork butt, with its gunmetal ferrule and reel rings and the exquisite frail slenderness of two top joints.

'It's got two top joints – two!' I exclaimed ecstatically.

'Of course,' said he. 'All good trout rods have two.'

I marvelled in silence at what seemed to me then a combination of extravagance and excellent precaution.

There must have been something inherently understanding and noble about that young man who would one day be my uncle, for, taking me by the arm, he sat me down on a tuft of heather and took the pieces of rod from the case and fitted them together.

The rest of the company moved on and left me in paradise.

It is thirty-five years ago since that moment and not one detail of it is forgotten. There sounds in my ears today as clearly as then the faint, clear pop made by the little cork stoppers with their boxwood tops as they were withdrawn. I remember how, before fitting the pieces together, he rubbed the ferrules against the side of his nose to prevent them sticking. I remember looking up the length of it through a tunnel of sneck rings to the eyelet at the end. Not until he had fixed a reel and passed a line through the rings did he put the lovely thing into my hand.

So light it was, so firm, so persuasive; such a thing alive – a sceptre. I could do no more than say 'Oo!' and again, 'Oo!'

'A thrill, ain't it?' said he.

I had no need to answer that. In my new-found rapture was only one sorrow – the knowledge that such happiness would not endure, and that, all too soon, a blank and rodless future awaited me.

'They must be awfully – awfully 'spensive,' I said.

'Couple of guineas,' he replied off-handedly.

A couple of guineas! And we were poor folk and the future was more rodless than ever.

'Then I shall save and save and save,' I said.

And my imagination started to add up twopence a week into guineas. Two hundred and forty pennies to the pound, multiplied by two – four hundred and eighty – and then another twenty-four pennies – five hundred and four. Why, it would take a lifetime, and no sweets, no elastic for catapults, no penny novelty boxes or air gun bullets or ices or anything.

Tragedy must have been writ large upon my face, for he said suddenly, 'When's your birthday?'

I was almost ashamed to tell him how soon it was. Perhaps

he, too, was a little taken aback by its proximity, for that future uncle of mine was not so rich as uncles should be.

'We must see about it.'

'But it wouldn't – it couldn't be one like that,' I said.

I must have touched his pride, for he answered loftily, 'Certainly it will.'

In the fortnight that followed I walked on air and told everybody I had as 'good as got a couple-of-guineas rod'.

No one can deceive a child, save the child himself, and when my birthday came and with it a long brown paper parcel, I knew, even before I had removed the wrappers, that this two-guinea rod was not worth the money. There was a brown linen case, it is true, but it was not a case with a neat compartment for each joint, nor was there a spear in the flap. There was only one top instead of two, and there were no popping little stoppers to protect the ferrules from dust and injury. The lower joint boasted no elegant cork hand piece, but was a tapered affair coarsely made and rudely varnished.

When I fitted the pieces together, what I balanced in my hand was tough and stodgy rather than limber. The reel, which had come in a different parcel, was of wood. It had neither check nor brake, and the line overran and back-wound itself with distressing frequency.

I had not read and reread Gamages' price list without

knowing something of rods, and I did not need to look long at this rod before realising that it was no match to the one I had handled on the Grayshott Road.

I believe at first a great sadness possessed me, but very presently imagination came to the rescue. For I told myself that I had only to think that this was the rod of all other rods that I desired most and it would be so. And it was so.

Furthermore, I told myself that, in this great wide, ignorant world, but few people existed with such expert knowledge of rods as I possessed. That I had but to say, 'Here is the final word in good rods,' and they would accept it as such.

Very confidently I tried the experiment on my mother, with inevitable success. From the depths of her affection and her ignorance on all such matters she produced:

'It's a magnificent rod.'

I went my way, knowing full well that she knew not what she said, but that she was kind.

With rather less confidence I approached my father, saying, 'Look, father! It cost two guineas. It's absolutely the best sort you can get.'

And he, after waggling it a few moments in silence, quoted cryptically:

'There is nothing either good or bad, but thinking makes it so.'

Young as I was, I had some curiosity about words, and on

any other occasion I would have called on him to explain. But this I did not do, but left hurriedly, for fear that he should explain. In the two years that followed, I fished every day in the slip of a back garden of our tiny London house. And, having regard to the fact that this rod was never fashioned to throw a fly, I acquired a pretty knack in the fullness of time and performed some glib casting at the nasturtiums and marigolds that flourished by the back wall.

My parents' fortunes must have been in the ascendant, I suppose, for I call to mind an unforgettable breakfast when my mother told me that father had decided we should spend our summer holiday at a Welsh hotel on the river Lledr. The place was called Pont-y-pant, and she showed me a picture of the hotel with a great knock-me-down river creaming past the front of it.

Although in my dreams I had heard fast water often enough, I had never seen it, and the knowledge that in a month's time I should wake with the music of a cataract in my ears was almost more than patience could endure.

In that exquisite, intolerable period of suspense I suffered as only childish longing and enthusiasm can suffer. Even the hank of gut that I bought and bent into innumerable casts failed to alleviate that suffering. I would walk for miles for a moment's delight captured in gluing my nose to the windows of tackleists' shops in the West End.

I learned from my grandmother – a wise and calm old lady – how to make nets and, having mastered the art, I made myself a landing net. This I set up on a frame fashioned from a penny schoolmaster's cane bound to an old walking stick. It would be pleasant to record that this was a good and serviceable net, but it was not. It flopped over in a very distressing fashion when called upon to lift the lightest weight. I had to confess to myself that I had more enthusiasm than skill in the manufacture of such articles.

At school there was a boy who had a fishing creel, which he swapped with me for a Swedish knife, a copy of *Rogues of the Fiery Cross*, and an Easter egg which I had kept on account of its rare beauty.

He had forced a hard bargain and was sure he had the best of it, but I knew otherwise.

At last the great day dawned, and after infinite travel by train we reached our destination as the glow of sunset was greying into dark. The river was in spate, and as we crossed a tall stone bridge on our way to the hotel I heard it below me, barking and grumbling among great rocks. I was pretty far gone in tiredness, for I remember little else that night but a rod rack in the hall – a dozen rods of different sorts and sizes, with gaudy salmon flies, some nets, a gaff, and an oak coffer upon which lay a freshly caught salmon on a blue ashet. Then supper by candlelight, bed, a glitter of stars through the open window, and the ceaseless drumming of water.

By six o'clock next morning I was on the river bank, fitting my rod together and watching in awe the great brown ribbon of water go fleetly by.

Among my most treasured possessions were half a dozen flies, and two of these I attached to the cast with exquisite care. While so engaged, a shadow fell on the grass beside me and, looking up, I beheld a lank, shabby individual with a walrus moustache and an unhealthy face, who, the night before, had helped with our luggage at the station.

'Water's too heavy for flies,' said he, with an uptilting inflection. 'This evening, yes; now, no – none whateffer. Better try with a worrum in the burrun.'

He pointed at a busy little brook which tumbled down the steep hillside and joined the main stream at the garden end.

'C-couldn't I fish with a fly in the – burrun?' I asked, for although I wanted to catch a fish very badly, for honour's sake I would fain take it on a fly.

'Indeed, no,' he replied, slanting the tone of his voice skyward. 'You cootn't. Neffer. And that isn't a fly rod whateffer.'

'It is,' I replied hotly. 'Yes, it is.'

But he only shook his head and repeated, 'No,' and took

the rod from my hand and illustrated its awkwardness and handed it back with a wretched laugh.

If he had pitched me into the river I should have been happier.

'It is a fly rod and it cost two guineas,' I said, and my lower lip trembled.

'Neffer,' he repeated. 'Five shillings would be too much.'

Even a small boy is entitled to some dignity.

Picking up my basket, I turned without another word and made for the hotel. Perhaps my eyes were blinded with tears, for I was about to plunge into the dark hall when a great, rough, kindly voice arrested me with:

'Easy does it.'

At the thick end of an immense salmon rod there strode out into the sunlight the noblest figure I had ever seen.

There is no real need to describe my colonel again – I have done so already – but the temptation is too great. Standing in the doorway, the sixteen-foot rod in hand, the deerstalker hat, besprent with flies, crowning his shaggy head, the waders, like sevenleague boots, braced up to his armpits, the creel across his shoulder, a gaff across his back, he looked what he was – a god. His eyes met mine with that kind of smile one good man keeps for another.

'An early start,' he said. 'Any luck, old fellar?'

I told him I hadn't started – not yet.

'Wise chap,' said he. 'Water's a bit heavy for trouting. It'll soon run down through. Let's vet those flies of yours.'

He took my rod and whipped it expertly.

'A nice piece – new, eh?'

'N-not quite,' I stammered; 'but I haven't used it yet, sir, in water.'

That god read men's minds.

'I know – garden practice; capital; nothing like it.'

Releasing my cast, he frowned critically over the flies – a Blue Dun and a March Brown.

'Think so?' he queried. 'You don't think it's a shade late in the season for these fancies?' I said I thought perhaps it was. 'Yes, I think you're right,' said he. 'I believe in this big water you'd do better with a livelier pattern. Teal and Red, Cock-y-bundy, Greenwell's Glory.'

I said nothing, but nodded gravely at these brave names.

Once more he read my thoughts and saw through the wicker sides of my creel a great emptiness.

'I expect you've fished most in southern rivers. These Welsh trout have a fancy for a spot of colour.'

He rummaged in the pocket of his Norfolk jacket and produced a round tin which once had held saddle soap.

'Collar on to that,' said he; 'there's a proper pickle of flies and casts in that tin that, as a keen fisherman, you won't mind sorting out. Still, they may come in useful.'

14

'But, I say, you don't mean—' I began.

'Yes, go on; stick to it. All fishermen are members of the same club, and I'm giving the trout a rest for a bit.' His eyes ranged the hills and trees opposite. 'I must be getting on with it before the sun's too high.'

Waving his free hand, he strode away and presently was lost to view at a bend in the road.

I think my mother was a little piqued by my abstraction during breakfast. My eyes never for an instant deserted the round tin box which lay open beside my plate. Within it were a paradise and a hundred miracles all tangled together in the pleasantest disorder. My mother said something about a lovely walk over the hills, but I had other plans, which included a very glorious hour which should be spent untangling and wrapping up in neat squares of paper my new treasures.

'I suppose he knows best what he wants to do,' she said.

So it came about that I was left alone, and betook myself to a sheltered spot behind a rock where all the delicious disorder was remedied and I could take stock of what was mine.

I am sure there were at least six casts all set up with flies, and ever so many loose flies and one great stout, tapered cast, with a salmon fly upon it, that was so rich in splendour that I doubted if my benefactor could really have known

15

that it was there.

I felt almost guilty at owning so much, and not until I had done full justice to everything did I fasten a new cast to my line and go a-fishing.

There is a lot said and written about beginner's luck, but none of it came my way. Indeed, I spent most of the morning extricating my line from the most fearsome tangles. I had no skill in throwing a cast with two droppers upon it and I found it was an art not to be learned in a minute.

Then, from overeagerness, I was too snappy with my back cast, whereby before many minutes had gone I heard that warning crack behind me that betokens the loss of a tail fly. I must have spent half an hour searching the meadow for that lost fly and finding it not. Which is not strange, for I wonder has any fisherman ever found that lost fly. The reeds, the buttercups, and the little people with many legs who run in the wet grass conspire together to keep the secret of its hiding place.

I gave up at last, and with a feeling of shame that was only proper, I invested a new fly on the point of my cast and set to work again, but more warily.

In that hard racing water a good strain was put upon my rod, and before the morning was out it was creaking at the joints in a way that kept my heart continually in my mouth. It is the duty of a rod to work with a single smooth action and by no means to divide its performance into three sections of activity. It is a hard task for any angler to persuade his line austerely if his rod behaves thus.

When, at last, my father strolled up the river bank, walking, to his shame, much nearer the water than a good fisherman should, my nerves were jumpy from apprehension.

'Come along. Food's ready. Done any good?' he said.

Again it was to his discredit that he put food before sport, but I told him I had had a wonderful morning, and he was glad.

'What do you want to do this afternoon, old man?' he asked.

'Fish,' I said.

'But you can't always fish,' he said.

I told him I could, and I was right, and have proved it for thirty years and more.

'Well, well,' he said, 'please yourself, but isn't it dull not catching anything?'

And I said, as I've said a thousand times since, 'As if it could be.'

So that afternoon I went downstream instead of up, and found myself in difficult country where the river boiled between the narrows of two hills. Stunted oaks overhung the water and great boulders opposed its flow. Presently I came to a sort of natural flight of steps – a pool and a cascade three times repeated – and there, watching the maniac fury of the waters in awe and wonderment, I saw the most stirring sight in my young life.

I saw a silver salmon leap superbly from the cauldron below into the pool above. And I saw another and another salmon do likewise. And I wonder the eyes of me did not fall out of my head.

I cannot say how long I stayed watching that gallant pageant of leaping fish – in ecstasy there is no measurement of time – but at last it came upon me that all the salmon in the sea were careering past me and that if I were to realise my soul's desire I must hasten to the pool below before the last of them had gone by.

It was a mad adventure, for until I had discovered that stout cast, with the gaudy fly attached in the tin box, I had given no thought to such noble quarry. My recent possessions had put ideas into my head above my station and beyond my powers. Failure, however, means little to the young, and, walking fast, yet gingerly, for fear of of breaking my rod top against a tree, I followed the path downstream until I came to a great basin of water into which, through a narrow throat, the river thundered like a storm.

At the head of the pool was a plate of rock scored by the nails of fishermen's boots, and here I sat me down to wait while the salmon cast, removed from its wrapper, was allowed to soak and soften in a puddle left by the rain.

And while I waited a salmon rolled not ten yards from where I sat. Head and tail, up and down he went, a great monster of a fish, sporting and deriding me.

With that performance so near at hand, I have often wondered how I was able to control my fingers well enough to tie a figure-eight knot between the line and the cast. But I did, and I'm proud to be able to record it. Your true-born angler does not go blindly to work until he has first satisfied his conscience. There is a pride, in knots, of which the laity knows nothing, and if, through neglect to tie them rightly, failure and loss should result pride may not be restored nor conscience salved by the plea of eagerness.

With my trembling fingers I bent the knot, and with a pummelling heart, launched the line into the broken water at the throat of the pool.

At first the mere tug of the water against that large fly was so thrilling to me that it was hard to believe that I had not hooked a whale. The trembling line swung round in a wide arc into a calm eddy below where I stood. Before casting afresh I shot a glance over my shoulder to assure myself there was no limb of a tree behind me to foul the fly. And this was a gallant cast, true and straight, with a couple of yards more length than its predecessor, and a wide radius. Instinctively I knew, as if the surface had been marked with an X where the salmon had risen, that my fly must pass right over the spot. As it swung by, my nerves were strained like piano wires. I think I knew that something tremendous, impossible, terrifying was going to happen. The sense, the certitude was so strong in me that I half opened my mouth to shout a warning to the monster, not to.

I must have felt very, very young in that moment. I, who that same day had been talked to as a man by a man among men. The years were stripped from me and I was what I was – ten years old and appalled.

And then, with the suddenness of a rocket, it happened. The water was cut into a swathe. I remember a silver loop bearing downwards – a bright, shining, vanishing thing like the bobbin of my mother's sewing machine – and a tug. I shall never forget the viciousness of that tug. I had my fingers tight upon the line, so I got the full force of it. To counteract a tendency to go head first into the spinning water below, I threw myself backward and sat down on the hard rock with a jar that shut my teeth on my tongue – like the jaws of a trap.

Luckily I had let the rod go out straight with the line, else it must have snapped in the first frenzy of the down stream rush. Little ass that I was, I tried to check the speeding line with my forefinger, with the result that it cut and burnt me to the bone. There wasn't above twenty yards of line in the reel, and the wretched contrivance was trying to be rid of the line even faster than the fish was wrenching it out.

Heaven knows why it didn't snarl, for great loops and whorls were whirling, like Catherine wheels, under my wrist. An instant's glance revealed the terrifying fact that there were not more than half a dozen yards left on the reel, and the fish showed no sign of abating his rush. With the realisation of impending and inevitable catastrophe upon me, I launched a yell for help, which, rising above the roar of the waters, went echoing down the gorge.

And then, to add to my terrors, the salmon leaped – a swinging leap like a silver arch appearing and instantly disappearing upon the broken surface. So mighty, so all-powerful he seemed in that sublime moment that I lost all sense of reason and raised the rod, with a sudden jerk, above my head.

I have often wondered, had the rod actually been the two-guinea rod my imagination claimed for it, whether it could have withstood the strain thus violently and unreasonably imposed upon it. The wretched thing that I held so grimly never even put up a fight. It snapped at the ferrule of the lower joint and plunged like a toboggan down the slanting line, to vanish into the black depths of the water.

My horror at this calamity was so profound that I was lost even to the consciousness that the last of my line had run out. A couple of vicious tugs advised me of this awful truth. Then, snap! The line parted at the reel, flickered out through the rings, and was gone. I was left with nothing but the butt of a broken rod in my hand, and an agony of mind that even now I cannot recall without emotion.

I am not ashamed to confess that I cried. I lay down on the rock with my cheek in the puddle where I had soaked the cast, and plenished it with my tears. For what had the future left for me but a cut and burning finger, a badly bumped behind, the single joint of a broken rod, and no faith in uncles?

How long I lay there weeping I do not know. Ages, perhaps, or minutes, or seconds.

I was roused by a rough hand on my shoulder, and a kindly voice demanding, 'Hurt yourself, Ike Walton?'

Blinking away my tears, I pointed at my broken rod with a bleeding forefinger.

'Come! This is bad luck,' said my colonel, his face grave as a stone. 'How did it happen?'

'I c-caught a s-salmon.'

'You what?' he said.

'I d-did,' I said.

He looked at me long and earnestly; then, taking my injured hand, he looked at that and nodded.

'The poor groundlings who can find no better use for a

river than something to put a bridge over think all fishermen are liars,' said he. 'But we know better, eh? By the bumps and breaks and cuts I'd say you made a plucky fight against heavy odds. Let's hear all about it.'

So, with his arm round my shoulders and his great shaggy head near to mine, I told him all about it.

At the end he gave me a mighty and comforting squeeze, and he said, 'The loss of one's first big fish is the heaviest loss I know. One feels, whatever happens, one'll never—' He stopped and pointed dramatically. 'There it goes – see! Down there at the tail of the pool!'

In the broken water where the pool emptied itself into the shallows beyond I saw the top joints of my rod dancing on the surface.

'Come on!' he shouted, and gripping my hand, jerked me to my feet. 'Scatter your legs! There's just a chance!'

Dragging me after him, we raced along by the river path to the end of the pool, where, on a narrow promontory of grass, his enormous salmon rod was lying.

'Now,' he said, picking it up and making the line whistle to and fro in the air with sublime authority, 'keep your eyes skinned on those shallows for another glimpse of it.'

A second later I was shouting, 'There! There!'

He must have seen the rod point at the same moment, for his line flowed out and the big fly hit the water with a plop not a couple of feet from the spot.

He let it ride on the current, playing it with a sensitive touch like the brushwork of an artist.

'Half a jiffy!' he exclaimed at last. 'Wait! Yes, I think so. Cut down to that rock and see if I haven't fished up the line.'

I needed no second invitation and presently was yelling, 'Yes – yes, you have!'

'Stretch yourself out then and collar hold of it.'

With the most exquisite care he navigated the line to where I lay stretched upon the rock. Then:

'Right you are! Good lad! I'm coming down.'

Considering his age, he leaped the rocks like a chamois.

'Now,' he said, and took the wet line delicately between his forefinger and thumb. One end trailed limply downstream, but the other end seemed anchored in the big pool where I had had my unequal and disastrous contest.

Looking into his face, I saw a sudden light of excitement dancing in his eyes.

'Odd,' he muttered, 'but not impossible.'

'What isn't?' I asked breathlessly.

'Well, it looks to me as if the top joints of that rod of yours have gone downstream.'

Gingerly he pulled up the line, and presently an end with a broken knot appeared.

'The reel knot, eh?' I nodded gloomily. 'Then we lose the rod,' said he. That wasn't very heartening news. 'On the other hand, it's just possible the fish is still on – sulking.'

'Oo!' I exclaimed.

'Now, steady does it,' he warned, 'and give me my rod.'

Taking a pair of clippers from his pocket, he cut his own line just above the cast.

'Can you tie a knot?' he asked.

'Yes,' I nodded.

'Come on then; bend your line on to mine. Quick as lightning.'

Under his critical eye I joined the two lines with a blood knot. 'I guessed you were a fisherman,' he said, nodded approvingly, and clipped off the ends. 'And now to know the best or the worst.'

I shall never forget the music of that check reel or the suspense with which I watched as, with the butt of the rod bearing against the hollow of his thigh, he steadily wound up the wet slack line. Every instant I expected it to come drifting downstream, but it didn't. Presently it rose in a tight slant from the pool above.

'Snagged, I'm afraid,' he said, and worked the rod with an easy straining motion to and fro. 'Yes, I'm afraid – no, by Lord Bobs, he's on!'

I think it was only right and proper that I should have

launched a yell of triumph as, with the spoken word, the point at which the line cut the water shifted magically from the left side of the pool to the right.

'And a fish too,' said he.

In the fifteen minutes that followed, I must have experienced every known form of terror and delight.

'Youngster,' said he, 'you should be doing this by rights, but I'm afraid the rod's a bit above your weight.'

'Oh, go on and catch him,' I pleaded.

'And so I will,' he promised; 'unship the gaff, young un, and stand by to use it, and if you break the cast we'll never speak to each other again, and that's a bet.'

But I didn't break the cast. The noble, courageous, indomitable example of my river god had lent me skill and precision beyond my years. When at long last a weary, beaten, silver monster rolled within reach of my arm into a shallow eddy, the steel gaff shot out fair and true and sank home.

And then I was lying on the grass, with my arms round a salmon that weighed twenty-two pounds on the scale and contained every sort of happiness known to a boy.

And best of all, my river god shook hands with me and called me 'partner'.

That evening the salmon was placed upon the blue ashet in the hall, bearing a little card with its weight and my name upon it.

And I am afraid I sat on a chair facing it for ever so long, so that I could hear what the other anglers had to say as they passed by. I was sitting there when my colonel put his head out of his private sitting-room and beckoned me in.

'A true fisherman lives in the future, not the past, old man,' said he; 'though, for this once, it 'ud be a shame to reproach you.'

'We got the fish,' said he, 'but we lost the rod, and the future without a rod doesn't bear thinking of. Now' – and he pointed at a long wooden box on the floor, that overflowed with rods of different sorts and sizes – 'rummage among those. Take your time and see if you can find anything to suit you.'

'Oo, sir,' I said.

'Here, quit that,' he ordered gruffly. 'By Lord Bobs, if a show like this afternoon's don't deserve a medal, what does? Now, here's a handy piece by Hardy – a light and useful tool – or if you fancy greenheart in preference to split bamboo—'

I have the rod to this day, and I count it among my dearest treasures. And to this day I have a flick of the wrist that was his legacy. I have, too, some small skill in dressing flies, the elements of which were learned in his company by candlelight after the day's work was over. And I have countless memories of that month-long, month-short friendship – the closest and most perfect friendship, perhaps, of all my life.

He came to the station and saw me off.

How I vividly remember his shaggy head at the window, with the whiskered cheeks and the gunpowder marks at the corners of his eyes! I didn't cry, although I wanted to awfully. We were partners and shook hands. I never saw him again, although on my birthdays I would have coloured cards from him, with Irish, Scotch, Norwegian postmarks. Very brief they were: 'Water very low.' 'Took a good fish last Thursday.' 'Been prawning, but don't like it.'

Sometimes at Christmas I had gifts – a reel, a tapered line, a fly book. But I never saw him again.

Came at last no more postcards or gifts, but in the *Fishing Gazette*, of which I was a religious reader, was an obituary telling how one of the last of the Mutiny veterans had joined the great majority. It seems he had been fishing half an hour before he died.

So he was no more – my river god – and what was left to him they had put into a box and buried it in the earth.

But that isn't true; nor is it true that I never saw him again. For I seldom go a-fishing but that I meet him on the river banks.

The banks of a river are frequented by a strange company and are full of mysterious and murmurous sounds – the cluck and laughter of water, the piping of birds, the hum of insects, and the whispering of wind in the willows. What should prevent a man in such a place having a word and speech with another who is not there? So much of fishing lies in imagination, and mine needs little stretching to give my river god a living form.

'With this ripple,' says he, 'you should do well.'

'And what's it to be,' say I – 'Blue Upright, Red Spinner? What's your fancy, sir?'

Spirits never grow old. He has begun to take an interest in dry fly methods – that river god of mine, with his seven-league boots, his shaggy head, and the gaff across his back.